Welcome to the incredible world of the Night Zoo

Meet amazing magical creatures!

Follow Will's adventure as the Night Zookeeper

Beware of the evil army of Voids

Continue to explore the Night Zoo at nightzookeeper.com

Meet the Characters

Will

The Night Zookeeper, a force for good in a magical world that's under threat from an evil army of darkness.

Maji

A powerful and mysterious time-travelling elephant.

Riya

Fast, brave, impulsive. She never lets a silly thing like rules stand in her way.

Sam

Extremely tall and extremely clumsy, but when it comes to spying, he's the best.

The Voids

Robotic spiders set on destroying the Night Zoo and plunging it into darkness.

This book was co-written by Giles Clare

Illustrated by Dave Shephard, based
on original artwork by Buzz Burman

OXFORD
UNIVERSITY PRESS

Great Clarendon Street, Oxford OX2 6DP

Oxford University Press is a department of the University of Oxford.
It furthers the University's objective of excellence in research, scholarship,
and education by publishing worldwide. Oxford is a registered trade mark of
Oxford University Press in the UK and in certain other countries

Night Zookeeper material © Wonky Star Limited 2019
Text copyright © Oxford University Press 2019
Illustrations copyright © Wonky Star Limited 2019

The moral rights of the author have been asserted
Database right Oxford University Press (maker)

First published 2019

British Library Cataloguing in Publication Data

Data available

ISBN: 978-0-19-276408-9

1 3 5 7 9 10 8 6 4 2

Printed in Great Britain

Paper used in the production of this book is a natural,
recyclable product made from wood grown in sustainable forests.
The manufacturing process conforms to the environmental
regulations of the country of origin.

NIGHT ZOO KEEPER

The Elephant of Tusk Temple

Joshua Davidson

Illustrated by
Buzz Burman

OXFORD
UNIVERSITY PRESS

Chapter One

Will Rivers, the Night Zookeeper, stepped through the magic portal into a new part of the Night Zoo. His friends Riya and Sam the Spying Giraffe followed him through and emerged next to him. Will looked back at the closing portal. He gave a final wave to the animals of Igloo City on the other side.

Maji the elephant had appeared moments before. She had told him to hurry to the Tusk Temple. She hadn't said why, but Will knew in his heart that it must important. As the portal disappeared, he turned away from the sparkling ice of Igloo City to face a large, lush garden.

'Aaaahh, that's better,' said Sam. He wiggled his feet in the soft grass and sighed with pleasure. 'I can feel my hooves again.'

Will unbuttoned his zookeeper's coat.
He too was relieved to leave the cold behind.
He drew a deep breath in through his nose.
The air was warm and sweet-smelling.

'You're right, Sam,' he said. 'What a beautiful place.'

The three friends were standing on a grassy path that stretched away in front of them. There were box hedges like green walls to their left and right. Even Sam wasn't quite tall enough to see over the tops of the hedges. There were long, neat beds full of glowing, colourful flowers along the foot of each hedge. The intoxicating scent from the flowers filled their nostrils.

Riya nodded in approval. 'Wow! Do you think we've come somewhere that isn't full of danger for a change?' she asked with a wry smile.

'Oh, yes, I think so,' replied Sam with a contented yawn. 'Look. There it is: Tusk Temple.'

Will and Riya looked straight ahead down the long grassy path. Way in the distance, part of a huge purple building was visible over the top of the hedges. Two enormous columns like curved white tusks supported a roof that was shaped like an elephant's forehead and ears. In the centre of the temple roof was a large, glowing symbol.

Riya said, 'It's the infinity symbol, Will. That must be Maji's home.'

Will grinned. She was right. The glowing

shape was just like the one he had painted on the wall of the zoo. It was just like the one he drew with his torch to make the portals. 'Well, guys, what are we waiting for? Maji told us to meet her there,' said Will. 'Let's go!'

'And at least we know the way,' said Riya with a smile. 'Not much choice this time. Straight on it is.'

Will and Riya set off along the path at a trot. A few seconds later, Will noticed Sam wasn't with them. He stopped and turned around. Sam was standing with his front legs far apart and his neck and head lowered close to the ground. He was examining one of the flower beds with so much interest that he had been left behind.

'Hey, Sam, what are you doing?' Will called back.

'Yeah, come on, Sam, Maji told us to hurry,'

said Riya.

Sam turned his head to face them. 'But these flowers are amazing, even for the Night Zoo,' he replied. 'Please, just have a look.'

Will shrugged his shoulders at Riya. 'I guess a few minutes won't hurt,' he said. 'Let's see what he's found.'

Riya rolled her eyes. 'That giraffe has got you wrapped around his hoof,' she replied.

Will and Riya walked back to the stooping giraffe. They knelt beside him and looked at the luscious flower bed. A huge variety of flowers glowed in the soil, casting a rainbow of colours across their faces. There were flowers shaped like giant ice-cream cones, flaming tongues of fire, perfect crystal spheres, and luminous feathery wings. The three friends fell silent for a few seconds, mesmerized by the spectacular sight.

Sam broke the silence, 'Each one has a name, see. They're all labelled.' Will and Riya noticed a small plaque at the base of each plant. Will read some of the labels out loud, 'Fire Tulip . . . Wings of Paradise . . . Singing Rose . . . Violent Violet . . .'

Sam's eyes flew open. 'Violent Violet!' he repeated.

Riya frowned. 'Hmmm, maybe we shouldn't get too close.'

'Yeah, come on, we'd better move on,' said Will, standing up.

Sam rose to his full height. 'Hey, Riya,' he said.

Riya looked up at him. Sam was smirking. 'Oh no,' she groaned. She knew what was coming.

'Hey, Riya, why have you got some of those flowers on your face?' asked Sam, his dark eyes twinkling.

'Okay, I haven't got flowers on my face, but—'

'You have, you've got tulips!' chortled Sam. 'Geddit? Tulips. Two lips. Hahaha.'

Despite her best efforts, Riya giggled. 'You annoying,

high-rise horse,' she said and gave him a friendly thump on the leg.

Will laughed too. The atmosphere in the garden was so calm and relaxing that he felt the tension of their other adventures slipping away. And very soon, he knew they would be with Maji in her magnificent temple and they would be safe: safe from the Voids, the army of robot spiders terrorizing the Night Zoo; safe from the treacherous owl, Circles; safe from all the other dangers of the Night Zoo. Will felt a warm glow of contentment in his chest as he, Riya and Sam set off towards the temple.

'Ah, maybe this isn't going to be as simple as we thought,' said Riya.

They were facing another tall hedge. They had followed the path until they had come to a junction, where the path split left and right.

'But the temple's straight on,' complained Sam. 'Why would you put a stupid hedge in the way?'

'Sam, can you see over the top at all?' asked Will.

'I don't think so, but I'll have a go,' said the young giraffe. He placed his feet together, stood up on the tips of his hooves and raised his long neck as high as it would go.

His nostrils ended up in line with the top of the hedge, so that he could just peek over it. Sam wobbled and tottered.

'Can you see anything?' Will called up.

'Whoa, it's amazing!' yelled Sam.

'Sam, stop admiring the view and tell us what you can see,' said Riya.

'I just did!' protested Sam.

'What are you talking about? All you said was that it's amazing.'

'No, I didn't! I said it's a *maze* thing!'

'Oh,' said Riya. 'Right, got it. Sorry.'

'A maze?' asked Will. 'Can you see the way through to the temple?'

Sam strained his neck a few inches higher. 'No, not really, it's big and—OH!' Teetering on his hooves, Sam suddenly lost balance. He stumbled to one side and then the other. Will and Riya scrambled out of the way, but there wasn't much room with the hedges blocking them in. Sam, his legs twisted beneath him, spun on the spot. His long tongue flew out of his mouth and slapped Riya in the face before he collapsed in a heap.

Riya glared at Sam. Giraffe dribble was dripping from her chin. 'Unbelievable,' she muttered.

'Come on, you two,' said Will. 'We just have to take a guess.' He looked at the two paths going in opposite directions. 'Well, left or right?'

'Left,' said Sam.

'Right,' said Riya.

Will shook his head. 'I'll choose then.'

Sometime later, the three friends stood facing another high hedge and another left-right junction. Sam was peeping over the top of the hedge.

'The temple is straight ahead of us again. We might be a bit closer now, I'm not sure.'

'Argh, this is so frustrating,' said Will. 'We seem to be going in circles!'

'I thought we'd left Circles behind in Igloo City,' said Sam with a weak smile.

They continued further into the maze, turning this way and that, away from the temple and even back on themselves, until at last they spotted something different.

'Wow, look at those,' said Sam. Ahead the path widened, and on each side there were huge bushes that had been carefully cut into fantastical leafy statues.

Will approached the first one. It was a figure of an animal at least twenty feet tall. But it was like no animal he had ever seen. The top half was a rhino with a long, sharp horn but its bottom half was the powerful tail of a whale. The next plant statue had the head of a praying mantis, but the lithe body of a cheetah. There were dozens more lining the path ahead and Will and Riya wandered wide-eyed and silently amongst them.

'Hey, Sam,' said Riya. 'Here's some weird cousin of yours.' She was staring up at a beetle with a giraffe's head. 'Sam? Oh, what's he doing now?'

Will and Riya looked back at the young giraffe, who had his nose in a flower bed again.

'What's up, Sam?' Will called back.

Sam turned to face them. He was frowning. 'I don't know. There's something funny about these bushes. My ossicones are tingling.'

'Forget it, Sam,' said Will. 'We're wasting

time. Let's keep moving.' At that very moment, something moved in the flower bed next to Sam. 'Look out!' shouted Will. A long, thick, leafy vine shot out from the bed and wrapped itself around one of Sam's front legs. Sam looked down at it in alarm and tried to pull his leg away just as another vine whipped around his other leg.

'Help me!' cried the giraffe. Will and Riya charged back towards Sam, but more vines attacked Sam with the speed of striking snakes, each one coiling itself further around the giraffe's legs, chest and neck. Sam was rooted to the spot, unable to pull away as the vines enveloped him. Riya immediately grabbed at the vines, trying to pull them off with all her strength. Will tried the same, but the vines

only seemed to tighten their grip. He looked up at Sam, whose eyes were full of panic. The vine around Sam's neck was tightening so that the giraffe could only croak, 'Get them . . . off me!'

'Hang in there,' Will reassured him.

'Urgh, what *are* these things?' grunted Riya. She was on Sam's back yanking at a thick vine around his neck. A thought struck Will. Yes, what *were* these things? He ducked down to peer into the flower bed. The writhing vines were all coming from one plant. Will spotted the label: Silent Creeper. He glanced up at poor Sam, who was beginning to resemble one of the giant animal statues. Was it possible that all these strange creatures had been mummified by the vines? And now it was happening to Sam? Will shook the horrible thought from his mind. A Silent Creeper, he thought. How do you defeat something silent?

'Shout, Riya!' Will cried.

'What?'

'Shout! Scream, anything!'

'Okay!' Riya let go of the vines and leapt to the ground. 'Get off him! Get off!' she screamed at the top of her voice.

'Let him go!' roared Will with all his heart.

'Leave my friend alone!' screeched Riya.

The vines started to quiver. The one around Sam's neck loosened and slipped down. 'It's working! Louder!' Riya encouraged them. Sam joined in, bellowing with all his might. The three of them shouted and screamed at the tops of their voices. The vines became looser and looser until they finally released Sam and retreated into the flower bed.

'Sam, are you all right?' asked Will, hugging his friend's neck.

Sam nodded slowly. 'Thank you. That was '. . . creepy!' He turned and smiled at Riya. 'You said I was your friend,' he gushed. The tip of his glistening, blue tongue popped out between his lips.

'Oh, no! Don't even think about licking me, Clumsy Longlegs,' she warned.

Chapter Two

The three friends continued to work their way through the maze. From time to time, Sam peeked over the top of the hedges to help guide them. They hit several more dead ends and had to double-back and try different routes. All the time, the top of the enormous Tusk Temple was visible. Little by little, they seemed to be getting closer to it.

Will looked up at the bright infinity symbol on the temple roof. He found himself thinking about his grandma. Looking around at the weird and wonderful plant life, Will thought about how much his Grandma Rivers would love these gardens. It was just her sort of place: full of magic, mystery and statues of impossible animals. He wondered where Grandma Rivers had disappeared to on his birthday, the day he had entered the Night Zoo. 'Wherever you are, Grandma, I really wish you were here right now,' he said under his breath. He missed her strange stories and wise advice. As they trudged along the path,

Will noticed other reminders of home. There was a bush that was the same shape as the wonky birthday cake his brother Charlie had made him. There was a flower that looked like the Orb his grandma had given to him as a present before she disappeared. And there were even hanging baskets filled with plants that looked like the brass bell that hung outside Grandma Rivers' shed. He reached out and touched one gently; it swayed on its stem and tinkled just like his grandma's bell.

They turned a corner and Will's eyes lit up. 'At last!' exclaimed Riya. Just ahead, the tall hedges on either side of them came to an end.

They had found the exit to the maze! Two enormous tusks stood like sentries guarding the exit. Will dashed forwards and stroked the shimmering stone.

'We're coming, Maji,' he said. The sight in front of them was breath-taking. A line of stone tusks snaked across a wide clearing in the moon-drenched trees. Will's eyes followed the path of tusks all the way up to the foot of the magnificent Tusk Temple.

'Wow,' said Riya. 'Now that is impressive, right?'

Will could only nod in agreement. He couldn't explain it, but he suddenly felt as if he were closer to home than at any other time in the Night Zoo. It was a comforting feeling. He gave Riya a wide smile.

'Uh-oh,' said Sam suddenly. He was frozen

to the spot, frowning.

'What's up?' asked Will, still grinning.

'Is it one of your ice-cream cone alerts?' said Riya playfully.

Sam stuck the tip of his tongue out at her. 'No, but it is an *ossicone* alert,' he said. 'Whoa, now they're really jangling. There's something wrong, Will. I don't like this at all.'

Will looked at the path of tusks leading up to the temple. The leaves on the trees rustled gently in the night air. Apart from that, nothing was stirring under the peaceful moonlight. For a moment, he thought Sam's spying instincts were letting him down for once. Then, out of the corner of his eye, Will spotted something amongst a group of trees. There was something different about the light. The brilliant silvery moonlight had been replaced by a dull, red glow.

Riya had spotted it too. 'What's that? Maybe someone's lit a fire,' she said.

Sam was flicking his head about as if he were trying to shake off an angry wasp, 'Ow, that actually hurts,' he complained. 'My ossicones are really throbbing. Something big is coming, Will, something big and bad!'

Will peered through the trees at the red glow. It was increasing in strength. It was no fire, he realized. He gulped. He knew that crimson light all too well by now.

'Voids!' he said. 'And lots of them.'

Clicker-clacker!

Clicker-clacker!

'Quick, get out of sight,' said Will quietly. He hugged himself in tight next to the stone tusk. Riya dashed behind the other one.

'Sam, hide!' whispered Will.

'Where?' asked Sam in confusion, looking around for something big enough to hide behind.

'No, turn invisible!' Will urged. 'Quick!'

'Oh yeah, good idea,' replied Sam sheepishly. He closed his eyes, there was a brief, bright flash and suddenly the young giraffe disappeared.

The night air was filled with the clanking of metal limbs and the gnashing of razor-sharp fangs. The Voids appeared between the trees: a long column of the ugly robot spiders was approaching the clearing. Their red eyes pulsed in unison as they marched in pairs. Will watched as the lead Void reached one of the stone tusks. *Clicker-clacker! Clicker-clacker!* The Void stopped, then squirted thick, grey tar from its fangs all over the tusk. A second Void scuttled forwards and rammed the tusk with its metal head. The stone tusk cracked.

The Void rammed it again and this time it was ripped from the earth. It toppled slowly and then crashed to the ground, shattering into several chunks.

The army of Voids turned onto the path and marched on. Straight towards the temple!

Will clenched his jaw. 'We've got to get ahead of them,' he whispered over to Riya. 'Maji's in the temple, I'm sure. We've got to get there first.'

Riya nodded. 'We'll have to go around, through the trees, and hope they don't spot us,' she replied.

'Okay, let's go!'

Will, Riya and Invisible Sam ran through the trees as fast and as quietly as they could, dashing from tree to tree. Soon they were alongside the Voids, who plodded on robotically towards Tusk Temple, unaware of the children and the giraffe in the trees. The friends moved ahead, but twenty metres from the temple steps, the trees came to an end. Will and Riya hid behind the last one.

'How are we going to get inside without them seeing us?' panted Riya.

Will was looking back over his shoulder at the column of Voids, wondering the same thing. The Void army had halted again. Two of the Voids were hosing another tusk with sticky tar. The other Voids were all watching.

'They're distracted,' said Will. 'Go now!' Will and Riya charged across the clear ground and bounded up the steps. One of the towering wooden doors was open and they dashed for cover inside.

Invisible Sam followed, but as he tried to climb the steps, his hooves got in a tangle. 'Oh no!' he exclaimed. Sam tried to keep his balance but toppled over and landed in a heap. 'Oof!' he said. There was a bright flash and the young giraffe reappeared as clear as day on the temple steps.

Clicker-clacker! Clicker-clacker!

Will was at the doorway, watching in dismay. 'Get up, you clumsy giraffe, get in!' he urged his friend.

Sam clambered to his feet and skittered through the doorway, which was so tall even he didn't need to duck. Will looked back down the path. Hundreds of throbbing red eyes were glaring at him. There was a moment of stillness and then the Void army charged towards him.

Will stumbled backwards. 'Close the door,' he called out. 'Close the door!'

Will, Riya and Sam threw themselves against the huge temple door, but it was so heavy it barely moved an inch. 'Come on!' Will bellowed.

'It's . . . no . . . good,' said Riya, breathing hard.

Will whirled away and stuck his hand in his coat pocket. 'Maybe this will work,' he said. 'Step back, you two.' Will pulled out his torch, aimed and pressed the switch. The entrance chamber to the temple was lit up by the brilliant beam. Will concentrated as hard as he could, focusing on pushing the heavy door on its hefty hinges.

Clicker-clacker! The sound of the approaching Void army was so loud that the temple floor was trembling. Will's hand and arm ached as he struggled to control the shaking torch and its beam. Slowly, the temple door began to swing closed. Riya was staring through the gap, her eyes wide with fear. 'Hurry, Will, they're here!' she shouted above the din. Beams of crimson light shot in through the narrowing doorway and they all heard the scraping of sharp metal feet on the stone steps. Will grunted with effort as he clung onto the bucking torch. The giant door closed with a loud thud that echoed inside the temple. Will shut off the torch. For a second, there was silence . . .

Thump . . . thump, thump, thump!

The doors shuddered as Void after Void threw themselves against the outside. Will, Riya and Sam stepped back slowly. Will watched the juddering doors warily. Despite the Voids' violent efforts to smash through, the sturdy doors seemed to be holding. 'I think we're safe,' he said. As he spoke, the doors shook again and a stream of dust and grit trickled from the ceiling. Riya looked at Will in alarm. 'Well, safe for now,' he added. 'Let's get further into the temple.'

Chapter Three

Will, Riya and Sam turned away from the doors and followed a corridor into a huge room. The ceiling was held up by elegant stone pillars and the room was lit by flaming pink torches on the walls. The plants from the maze seemed to have crept inside and taken over. Beautiful patterns of orange, green, and purple moss swept

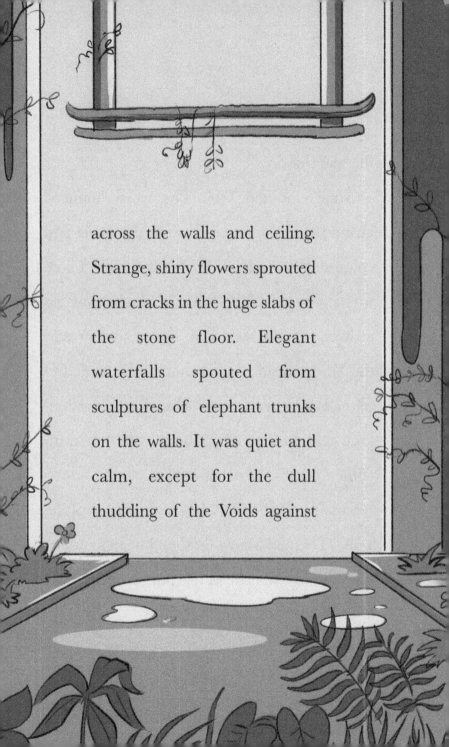

across the walls and ceiling. Strange, shiny flowers sprouted from cracks in the huge slabs of the stone floor. Elegant waterfalls spouted from sculptures of elephant trunks on the walls. It was quiet and calm, except for the dull thudding of the Voids against the giant doors.

'Maji!' shouted Will. The word bounced around the room, echoing off the walls and columns. 'We're here! Where are you?' There was no reply. 'Maji!' Again, there was no answer, just the sound of running water and the Voids outside the entrance. Will turned to Sam. 'I don't get it, Sam,' he said in frustration. 'You said this was Maji's home. She told us to come here. So, where is she?'

Sam nodded. 'Oh, this is the right place, Will. This is Maji's home, but it's not a question of *where* she is; it's more a question of *when* she is.'

Riya shot the giraffe a sideways look. 'Right, you're going to have to explain that one,' she said. 'And this better not be one of your stupid jokes.'

Sam shook his head. 'It's simple, Riya: Maji is the wisest and most powerful animal in the whole Night Zoo. She's a time-travelling elephant, for goodness' sake!'

'You mean she's not here because she might be travelling in time right now?' Riya asked, amazed.

'Exactly!' said Sam. 'In fact, they say anyone can travel in time in this temple! It's a mysterious and ancient place, full of secrets.'

'But it doesn't look like Maji or anyone else has been here for ages,' said Will. 'I mean, look around, guys.' He gestured towards the moss and flowers covering the walls and floor. Will couldn't help feeling cross. They had made it through the maze and only just escaped the Void army and now Maji wasn't even there to meet them. Where was she? Or *when* was she, as Sam had said? Will blew out his cheeks. 'Well, I guess we'd better look around for any clues,' he sighed.

The three of them split up to explore the room. Will wandered over towards one of the walls. He examined the moss to see if he could spot any writing or symbols. He couldn't make anything out. He moved on to one of the small waterfalls. The spouting water sparkled in the pink light, but there was nothing unusual or helpful here either. Will was about to turn away when he thought he saw something in the water. He looked more closely. There *was* something there, something just behind

the falling droplets: it was a man's face! Will wanted to step back, but he found he couldn't tear his eyes away. The face staring back at him was mostly covered by a grey metal mask with jagged edges. In fact, the whole of the man's face was grey: the skin of his lips, his ears, chin and eyelids, all of it grey. But it wasn't the lifeless colour that scared Will, it was the unblinking, coal-black eyes that bored into his own. There was something awful, something draining, about those eyes. Will could almost feel them sucking the energy from him. With great effort, Will twisted his head away. It was like trying to pull two strong magnets apart. The bond broke and Will stumbled backwards and tripped onto his backside. His heart was thumping in his chest and he was taking quick, shallow breaths. He glanced up nervously at the stream of water. The masked man had disappeared.

'Will, are you okay?' asked Riya. She trotted up next to him and held out her hand. He took it and she helped him to his feet. 'What just happened?'

'I . . .' he began. 'I think I . . .' He stopped. Will suddenly realized he had seen the masked face before. Back in the Fire Desert when he was ill, the same face had appeared in a dream. For reasons he didn't understand, Will found that he didn't want to tell Riya what he had just seen. This face kept appearing to him. It was personal and it didn't feel right to mention it. 'I . . . I think I just slipped,' he replied.

'Now who's the clumsy one?' said Sam with a cheeky grin.

There was an almighty thud. The whole temple seemed to shake. More dust and grit fell from the ceiling. The three friends stared back towards the temple entrance. The Voids must be attacking the doors with all their might.

'We need to find another way out of here,' said Riya. 'There's some more steps right on the other side, see over there by the torches.'

Boom! The stone slabs beneath their feet

trembled as they ran across the huge room. For the first time, Will wondered if the temple doors could survive the attack. They sprinted towards a pair of pink torches at the foot of some steps. *Crash!* A stone the size of a football smashed onto the floor a few feet in front of Will. He could only imagine what the Voids were doing to the outside of the temple; whatever it was, the temple was taking enough damage to knock stones loose from the ceiling. He leapt over it and ran on. He simply had to find Maji before it was too late.

'Look! A door . . . I think,' said Riya.

At the top of the steps, there was an unusual

double doorway. It was shaped like the infinity symbol, with one door directly above the other. The frames around the doors suddenly glowed purple. There was a whooshing sound as the doors spun like the hands of a clock and became a glittering blur. After a few seconds, they slowed again and came to a rest.

'Wow, it reminds me of those sand timer things,' said Riya.

Sam frowned. 'What's a sand timer? I didn't see them in the Fire Desert.'

'We've got them at school,' she explained. 'They're used to measure time—' Her face lit up. 'Time, Will! It must be some sort of time machine!'

Will nodded and smiled at her. 'Maji!' he said happily. He marched straight towards the bottom door. As he approached, it slid open automatically. It was dark beyond, but Will was

so sure that Maji would be there that he walked straight across the threshold. Sam and Riya stepped forwards to join him at the same time. Riya cried out in pain, 'Ow! You stepped on my foot again, you hapless hippo.' She stopped to rub her toes.

'Sorry,' said Sam.

Riya sighed. 'It's okay, just try—oh no!'

In front of them, the door slid closed. The infinity symbol glowed purple and the doors spun, taking Will away to who knew where or when.

Chapter Four

The door to the spinning room slid open and Will stepped out into a place he knew so well: he was on the path leading to the back garden of his own house. He was home! It was night time, but the downstairs lights were glowing, welcoming him back. He almost broke into a sprint for the steps. He felt a desperate urge to throw open the back door and fling himself into the arms of his mum and dad. His eyes lit up as he heard a familiar voice around the corner.

'Grandma! I'm here,' he spluttered as he dashed forwards. Will rounded the corner and skidded to a halt. There were two young boys sitting on the grass in front of Grandma Rivers's shed. Under a string of fairy lights, Grandma Rivers herself was perched on the steps of her shed talking to the children. Strangely, she hadn't even looked up when Will had appeared.

Will peered at the two boys. The smaller one was his younger brother, Charlie. Charlie smiled at something his grandma was saying and Will noticed Charlie's front teeth were missing. Will shook his head in disbelief. 'What?' he said. 'It's not possible.' Charlie had lost his baby front teeth ages ago and now had his adult ones. Will looked at the other boy and his stomach lurched with a mix of surprise and fright. The other boy sitting on the grass was him. He was staring at himself, but a couple of years younger. Will's legs felt a bit wobbly. 'Hello?' he said. His throat was so dry that it was barely a whisper. 'Hello? Grandma?' he repeated. Grandma Rivers, Charlie and his younger self ignored him. Will wondered why they hadn't noticed him. He was about to take a small step forwards when he felt a gentle tap on his shoulder. Will turned and nearly jumped out of his skin. He was face to face with a huge purple trunk.

'Hello, Night Zookeeper,' said Maji.

'Maji!' Will cried in relief, wrapping his arms around the elephant's trunk. 'I came to the temple like you said, but you weren't there,' he garbled, 'and now I seem to be home, but I'm not sure where or *when* I am, to be honest, any more!'

The huge purple elephant chuckled. 'Don't worry, my dear Will, this must be very strange for you. I expect you've got lots of questions!' Will nodded and looked up at Maji's magnificent broad head. The infinity symbol on her forehead was glowing gently and her wise, mischievous eyes twinkled in the fairy lights. Will had a hundred questions for her, but he couldn't think which one to start with. Maji smiled. 'Let's start with where we are,' she suggested. 'Or rather, when. By the way, they can't hear us, Will, because we are behind the curtain of time. Look carefully, just ahead. Do you see it now?'

Will turned back towards the others and squinted at the air just a few inches from his nose. There was a faint shimmering in the night air, like a gossamer-thin sheet of sparkling crystals hanging between him and the others. Instinctively, he reached out to touch it, but Maji gently slid the tip of her trunk around his wrist to stop him. She chuckled again. 'Sorry, my dear, but I must advise you not to touch it: you would give your younger self a terrible shock if he saw us.'

Will lowered his hand. 'I don't understand, Maji. Why am I here? This is the past, right? But the temple is under attack right now and Sam and Riya, they're in danger.'

Maji nodded. 'You are right, Will, but I brought you here to listen. Do you remember this moment?'

Will shook his head. 'I don't think so. Listen to what, Maji?'

'Your grandma,' she replied. 'Listen to what

she's telling you.'

Will turned to listen to Grandma Rivers.

'The Night Zoo is full of amazing, magical animals,' she was explaining. 'There are bumbling bees, polar wolves, and flamingos who work in hospitals, penguins who love hot chocolate and even tapirs that play tubas!'

'Are there giraffes?' asked Charlie.

'Oh, I'm sure there are,' she replied. 'But not just ordinary giraffes, of course. Special ones. What do you imagine is special about the giraffes, Will?'

Younger Will sat for a moment then shrugged his shoulders. 'Don't know,' he replied. 'I can't think of anything.'

Standing behind the curtain of time, Will almost laughed: it was so strange hearing himself talk, especially as his voice sounded higher.

'Now, I know that's not true, Will,' his grandma was saying. 'You have an amazing imagination. You just need to put it to work.'

Younger Will thought again then blew out his cheeks. 'The giraffes . . . they're tall, super tall,' he suggested.

Grandma Rivers nodded. 'That's a good start,' she said. 'Remember, you can create anything in the Night Zoo. You just have to believe. Have another go.'

Younger Will shifted uncomfortably on his bottom. 'The giraffes are special because . . . because they're tall . . . because . . . I don't know. I can't do it.'

'That's okay, Will,' said his grandma. 'It's not easy sometimes, is it? Sometimes you just have to work at things. Remember, persistence is the key.'

'They're spies!' cried Charlie. Younger Will sighed and his head dropped. 'They're Spying Giraffes and they live in Whispering Wood and their leader's called Nneka and there's a funny, clumsy one called Sam,' blurted out

Charlie enthusiastically.

'Wonderful!' said Grandma Rivers. 'What an imaginative leap, Charlie!'

Behind the curtain of time, Will could hardly believe his own ears. 'Sam! The giraffes! But they're real!' he exclaimed.

Maji nodded and said, 'Yes, they are. Now put your hand on my forehead, Will. It's time to visit another time.'

Will glanced back at his grandma, his brother and his younger self: Younger Will looked glum and it triggered a memory in Will now. He remembered this moment and how he had been a bit annoyed with Charlie for coming

up with a great idea. But more than that, he remembered how he had been annoyed with himself for giving up.

His fingertips touched the infinity symbol on Maji's forehead and Will was back in the spinning room bathed in beautiful purple light. A few seconds later, the door opened again and Will stepped out. Maji was already there, watching a different scene beyond the curtain of time. Will stood next to her.

'Remember this?' asked Maji with a smile.

'This was just the other day! Just before I came into the Night Zoo,' Will answered. He remembered it clearly. He saw himself again, but this time by the zoo wall. He was standing, paintbrush in hand, in front of his purple painting of Maji. Will watched

as Grandma Rivers talked to him and then pulled him into a powerful hug and whispered something in his ear.

'And do you remember what she said?' asked Maji.

'She told me I was ready. Finally ready. And I remember thinking, ready for what? Maji, what did my grandma mean? What am I ready for?' asked Will.

'Ready for what is coming next, Will,' said Maji. He could sense the seriousness in her tone. 'Because you have an incredible power, Night Zookeeper, and the Night Zoo needs you. Whatever you can imagine comes to life in the World of Night. Just like Charlie created Sam the Spying Giraffe, you created me.' Will stared at Maji in astonishment. 'That's right. Look at your amazing, original painting. You created me with your imagination. The Night

Zoo is full of your creations, but as you know, we are under attack. The Lord of Nulth has declared war on imagination and will not rest until we are nothing but dust. You've seen the damage his Voids can do. The Night Zoo is all that's left of the World of Night and it is shrinking by the second. But you, Will, you can save this place. You have the power to bring light back to the Night Zoo and stop the Lord of Nulth. It all starts here, Will. In the temple. You must face some trials and discover what it really means to be a Night Zookeeper.'

Before Will could respond, the infinity symbol on Maji's head glowed brightly and the scene in front of them fast-forwarded in time. Night fell in seconds and Will saw himself standing again in front of the glowing, magical gates about to enter the Night Zoo for the first time.

'Just remember, anything is possible in the Night Zoo,' said Maji next to him. She wrapped her trunk around him and gave him a powerful hug. 'All you have to do is believe. Touch my forehead again, my dear.'

'Where are we going now?' Will asked, reaching up to touch her forehead. As his fingers made contact, she replied, 'It's your time to shine.'

'Wait!' said Will, realizing what she meant, but the symbol glowed and Will was in the spinning room again. Seconds later, he tumbled out of the door and back into the temple.

'Will,' cried Riya, rushing forwards. 'Where have you been? Are you okay?'

Will felt slightly dizzy from all his time-travelling. He tried to clear his head, but he couldn't think how to explain.

Sam was grinning at him. 'You saw her, didn't you?' he beamed. 'You saw Maji!' Will nodded. 'What did she say? What did she say?' Sam was bouncing up and down with excitement. Riya swiftly moved out of range of his clattering hooves.

'Not much really,' replied Will. Riya and Sam both gave him a quizzical look. 'Only that I have to face the Night Zookeeper trials and save the temple. And then I have to save the Night Zoo, oh and then the entire world!' Will smiled weakly at his friends.

'Woohoo!' said Riya, grinning back at him. 'Now you're talking! Which way to the trials?' Riya rubbed her hands together enthusiastically. The sand timer doors spun again but this time they turned a brilliant yellow colour. When they stopped, a new door appeared with a large golden seal on it. 'Well, I guess that answers my question,' Riya said. 'Look, Will, it's the same symbol as the badge on your cap.'

The new door opened. Will took a deep breath. He had no idea what lay ahead, but he knew it was going to test them all. At that moment, they heard splintering, creaking wood, and a huge crash echoed through the room.

'Uh-oh,' said Sam, glancing back towards the entrance. Riya looked at Will in alarm.

No time to waste, thought Will grimly. The Voids had broken through. It was time to face the trials and save the temple.

Chapter Five

'**O**w!' complained Sam, banging his head on the way through the door. It immediately slid closed behind them. In fact, the door vanished completely into the wall. Will looked around the new, smaller room. It was circular and lit by more pink torches. He frowned.

'Can you guys see a way out?' he asked. He

could still hear rumbling and crashing back in the main chamber.

Riya walked around the outside of the room, running her hand along the wall. There were more infinity symbols painted on the stony surface, but otherwise it was smooth and there was no sign of an exit. 'Sorry, nothing,' she confirmed.

'Hey, look at this,' said Sam. He was in the middle of the room standing over a square table. There was a large model sitting on it, sealed in a glass box.

'It's a model of a maze,' said Riya. She squatted down. 'Look, here's the entrance.'

She pointed to a small hole in the face of the glass.

'It's not just a maze,' said Will, examining it closely. 'It's *the* maze. The same one that's outside the temple!'

'You're right,' said Sam, grinning. 'That's—'

'A-MAZE-ING!' interrupted Riya. She winked at Sam. 'Ha! Beat you to it.' Sam scowled at her.

Will was examining something at the centre of the model: there was a dome-shaped object with a key symbol engraved on it. 'I think I've found the way out,' he said. 'All we need to do is press that button.'

'But how do we get to it?' asked Riya. 'It's
sealed under the glass.'

'Smash it?' suggested Sam.

'But with what?' Riya replied.

'Reach inside somehow?' said Will, puzzled.

'I can't get my fingers past the entrance,'
said Riya, shaking her head.

'I could try sticking my tongue in,' said Sam.

Riya wrinkled her nose.

'It's all right. I've got a better idea,' said Will. He pulled out his torch. 'I managed to push the temple door closed with this. It should be easy enough to push a little button.' Will aimed the torch at the centre of the miniature maze and pressed the torch switch.

The brilliant beam shot out but reflected off the glass, scattering blinding light in all directions. Riya shielded her face in the crook of her elbow.

'Argh! Turn it off, turn it off!' urged Sam.

Will lowered the torch and blinked to clear his patchy vision. He blew out his cheeks. 'Well, that was a bright idea,' he muttered.

'You're telling me,' said Sam, rubbing his eyes with a hoof. 'Way too bright.'

'How about the Orb, Will?' suggested Riya. 'It helped you come up with ideas before.'

'As long as they're not bright ones,' grumbled Sam.

Suddenly, the floor shook and a stream of dust fell from the ceiling.

'The Voids are definitely inside the temple now,' said Riya. 'You'd better hurry, Will.'

Will pulled the Orb his grandma had given him from his pocket. He closed his eyes and raised it to his forehead. The grey, swirling

clouds inside the sphere immediately burst into a rainbow of colours. Will took slow, steady breaths. He was aware of heavy thuds and booms outside, but he tried to clear his mind of the distractions. An image started to form inside the Orb and his mind's eye. An object he recognized came into focus: it was a giant cup of steaming hot chocolate. Will noticed something strange scuttling about on the rim of the cup. It was a tiny animal. Will only just got a good look at it before the image grew faint and the colours in the Orb faded. Will opened his eyes and frowned.

'Well, what did you see?' asked Riya.

'I saw that huge mug of hot chocolate from Igloo City,' Will said, and paused.

'Is that it?'

'No, there was something else,' he said slowly. 'There was a tiny animal, just like one of the plant statues we saw in the maze garden. You know, the beetle one with the giraffe's head. It was on the rim of the mug.' He paused again. His mind was turning over, looking for a connection.

'How nice,' said Sam with a sigh. 'To be so small. Sometimes I get fed up with being so tall.'

Will's eyes widened as an idea sparked into

life in his mind. 'Oh!' he said. 'I think I get it now! Do you remember when I used the torch to make the mug of hot chocolate much bigger?' Riya and Sam both nodded. 'Well, perhaps I can do the opposite,' Will continued. He grinned up at Sam. 'You know, make things much smaller.'

'You mean . . . you mean shrink the model?' said Sam, grinning back. 'Great idea! Hang on . . . why?'

Will patted Sam on his chest. 'No, Sam, not the maze . . . you!' Sam blinked at him. 'So you can reach the button in the maze,' explained Will.

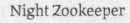

Sam looked from Will to
the model and back to Will.
And then he beamed
from ear to ear and
before Will could
stop him, Sam's long,
slippery tongue slithered
up the side of Will's face.
'Yes, oh yes!' cried Sam.
'Do it! Make me tiny!'

'Are you sure about this?' asked Will, wiping
away giraffe saliva with the sleeve of his coat.

Sam nodded vigorously.

'Rather you than me,' said Riya.

90

'Okay then, stand still,' said Will. 'Here goes!'

Will turned on the torch and Sam was bathed in bright light. 'Ooo! That tickles,' he giggled. Will focused his mind, imagining Sam growing smaller and smaller, but it was difficult to concentrate. Will's nerves were on edge: he had managed to make the mug bigger, but he had never tried anything like this on a living creature before, especially a friend. The torch shook in his hand and Will could feel the sweat on his palms. He clenched his jaw.

'Nothing's happening,' said Riya quietly. Sam was still stood full-size in the torch beam.

Will's hand and wrist were already aching. At that moment, a huge crash outside the room startled him and he released the button. Will found he was breathing faster than normal.

'What's wrong?' asked Riya.

'I don't know,' replied Will, flexing his sore fingers. 'It's too hard. I can't concentrate.'

Sam lowered his head to look straight into Will's eyes. 'Keep trying, Will. Don't worry about me. Just keep trying.'

'Sam's right,' agreed Riya. 'Try again, Will. This must be part of the trial.'

Will took a deep breath and turned on the torch. Again, in his mind's eye, he pictured

Sam shrinking. Wrapped in bright light, Sam exclaimed, 'Okay, this time something's happening!' Sam began to shrink all over. The torch bucked, Will's hand throbbed and his head was now aching. He was losing focus again. Sam stopped shrinking. Or rather, some of Sam stopped shrinking. Sam's long neck continued to shrink. 'Uh-oh,' said Sam, his head lowering towards his shoulders. At the same time, Sam's tail and ossicones were growing longer and longer. As Will lost concentration even more, Sam's back legs grew taller and his front legs grew shorter. Finally, Will was forced to release the torch button. In the pink light of the room, Riya and Will stared at Sam, their mouths open.

'Well, this is embarrassing,' muttered Sam, his head sitting on his shoulders and his bum way up in the air. His tail drooped to the floor and his ossicones were six feet tall. Riya was trying her best not to giggle.

'Oh no, Sam, I'm so sorry!' said Will in dismay. 'It's not funny, Riya! I can't do this!'

'Sorry, you're right,' she said. She examined Sam. 'Let's look at this positively: it's a good start.'

A good start, thought Will. Where had he heard that before? Of course, he thought, Grandma Rivers had said the same thing when he had been behind the curtain of time. Maji had shown him that particular moment for a reason, hadn't she? She'd told him to listen to his grandma. What else had Grandma Rivers said? It must have been something important . . . and then Will thought he understood. He remembered his grandma's exact words: *Sometimes you just have to work at things. Remember, persistence is the key.* It was clear to Will now. This was a trial after all, and trials weren't supposed to be easy.

'I'm not giving up this time,' he said firmly and lifted the torch again.

'Hang in there, Sam,' encouraged Riya.

The torch rattled the bones in Will's fingers and the muscles in his arms began to burn. His head throbbed and a droplet of sweat trickled down his brow. But, through it all, Will focused on his imagination and slowly Sam returned to the correct proportions and then began to shrink. The young giraffe grew smaller and smaller until a minute later, Riya called out, 'That's it! It's done!' Will turned off the torch, panting and massaging his aching arm. 'Oh, wow,' said Riya, kneeling on the floor, 'You're so cute and dinky!'

Sam the Shrunken Spying Giraffe was only five centimetres tall! He looked up at Riya, looming over him like a giant. 'I've changed my mind,' he said in a tiny, squeaky voice. 'I like being tall.'

Will knelt beside Riya. 'I'll change you back as soon as possible, buddy,' he said. 'Now, can you climb onto my hand?'

Sam clambered onto Will's outstretched palm and Will carefully lifted him up. 'Whoa, heights, don't like heights!' Sam moaned, peering over the side of Will's hand. Will carried Sam carefully to the entrance of the miniature maze.

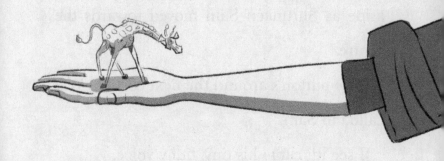

'You ready?' asked Will. Sam nodded and stepped inside. 'All right, we can see the way through the glass. Just follow our directions, okay?'

Will and Riya guided Sam along the corridors of the model maze. Meanwhile, the room rumbled with the force of the Voids' attack. Pebbles dropped from the ceiling onto the glass box. Riya quickly brushed them aside as Shrunken Sam moved towards the centre.

'The button's around the next corner,' Will called to Sam.

'I see it!' came his tiny, tinny voice.

'Hurry, Sam. Press it!' urged Riya.

Sam placed his two front hooves on the domed button. Nothing happened. It wouldn't move. He pressed again. 'I'm not heavy enough,' he shouted.

'Use all your weight,' Will called down to him. 'Sit on it or something!'

Sam turned around and lowered his backside onto the button. There was a click and purple light illuminated the key symbol on the button. At the same time, several of the infinity symbols on the walls began to glow as well, forming an archway. There was a click and the scraping of stone as a hidden door slid open.

'You did it, Sam!' cried Riya. Another crash shook the room. 'Come on. Get out of there. Run! That's it. Left, now right, keep going!'

Sam followed Riya's instructions and galloped through the maze back to the entrance, where Will held out his hand. Sam stepped into Will's palm. The floor shook violently and a crack appeared in the ceiling. Will cupped his other hand over the top of Sam. 'Sorry, no time to make you big again,' he said. 'The Voids are breaking through. Hang on!'

The Elephant of Tusk Temple

As grit and dust streamed from the ceiling, Will and Riya dashed across to the glowing archway and plunged through the exit.

Chapter Six

With Sam cupped safely in his hands and followed by Riya, Will emerged into another long corridor. Again, the door slid closed behind them and disappeared into the wall.

'Hey, it's dark in here,' came Sam's tiny voice. 'Can you make me big again, please?'

'Sure,' said Will, stooping to release Sam

onto the floor. Will lifted the torch, but Riya caught him by the arm.

'Hang on,' she said with a smirk. 'Sam, we'll make you tall again as long as you promise not to tell any more jokes, got it?'

'What? That's not fair!' squeaked the giraffe.

'Promise!' said Riya.

'Alright, alright!' huffed Sam.

Will switched on the torch and imagined Sam growing back to his full height. Slowly but surely, Sam returned to normal.

'Ahhh! That's better,' sighed Sam, stretching. He raised his neck up as high as he could and banged his ossicones on the ceiling. 'Ow!' he groaned.

'Good to have you back, Sam,' said Will with a wry smile.

The three companions followed the corridor.

'Will, I'm curious. What happened when you saw Maji?' asked Riya.

'It was amazing. She took me back in time,' explained Will. 'She showed me a moment in my past when I'd given up on something. Grandma Rivers was telling me that persistence is the key.

That's how I knew I had to keep trying to make Sam small.'

'Wow! You saw your grandma in the past?' said Riya.

'Not just her. I was behind a curtain in time and I saw Charlie and I even saw myself!'

'That must have been weird!'

Will nodded.

'I said you could time-travel in this temple,' said Sam smugly. 'That reminds me . . .'

'Reminds you what?' asked Will.

Sam gave them a goofy look and said, 'Knock, knock.'

'Noooo,' groaned Riya. 'You promised!'

'Haha, I had my ossicones crossed,' said Sam and stuck his tongue out at her. 'Come on, knock, knock!'

'Who's there?' answered Will.

'A time-traveller.'

'A time-traveller who?'

'Knock, knock!' cried Sam. 'Hahaha! Knock, knock! Geddit? He's a time-traveller. Haha! He's gone back in time and knocked again!'

Riya giggled despite herself and then burst out laughing. 'Alright, lanky legs, I admit that was quite a good one!'

Sam beamed with pride. 'Wanna hear another?'

'Hey, look,' said Will, interrupting. The corridor opened into another chamber lit by more torches with purple flames. There was another tall door ahead.

'At least there's an obvious way out this time,' said Sam.

'Yeah, but how do we get across *that*?' asked Will, pointing to a huge gap in the floor. 'There's no way we can jump across.'

'Trial number two?' suggested Riya.

They walked to the edge and looked down into a massive ravine: the sheer rocky walls dropped away into darkness way below. Sam swooned and his legs wobbled. Will looked around for a way across. Apart from a fallen few rocks and some vines criss-crossing the ceiling, the room was empty. It was then that he noticed some words engraved on the floor under his feet. 'Make an imaginative leap,' he read aloud.

'I bet you've got to *imagine* a way across, Will,' said Riya.

'As long as it doesn't involve bright ideas and heights,' said Sam, his legs still quivering.

Will smiled. 'Don't worry, Sam. I know what to do. It worked last time. I'll use the Orb again, obviously.'

'No, no, wait,' Sam grinned. '*Orb*viously!

Geddit? Orb-viously! Haha!'

'Just when I thought your jokes were improving,' Riya muttered.

Will held the Orb up to his forehead and closed his eyes. The grey clouds swirled inside but didn't light up. Will squeezed his eyelids shut and cleared his mind. Again, nothing happened inside the Orb or his mind's eye. No image emerged. No idea formed. Will lowered the Orb. 'It's not working,' he said quietly. He grabbed his torch. 'I'm sure this will show us something,' he said, trying not to sound worried. He held down the button. The beam came on for a spilt second and then flashed and spluttered. The torch went out. Will tried again. 'Come on,' he said through gritted teeth. Nothing happened this time. There was no light from the torch at all.

The three friends stood in silence for a few moments.

'Definitely trial number two,' said Riya.

Will chewed his bottom lip. Without his magical Orb and torch, he suddenly felt helpless. How was he supposed to work out what to do? He couldn't come up with any ideas without them. He read the words on the floor again: *make an imaginative leap*. A thought struck him: he remembered something about the huge mug of hot chocolate he had made for the penguins in Igloo City. He realized he hadn't used the Orb to come up with that idea. It had just come to him. He peered down into the depths of the ravine and Grandma Rivers' words seemed to echo in the darkness below: *You have an amazing imagination. You just need to put it to work.* Maybe she's right, he thought, maybe I am full of ideas, hidden away inside me, and I just need to reach down and grab one. He glanced up and instantly an idea hit him. The vines! If only his torch was working, he could use them to make a bridge. He heard Grandma River's voice again: *All you have to do is believe.* Will stared up at the network of vines. Was it possible? he wondered. Did he just have to believe?

'Will, are you okay?' said Sam. 'You're being really quiet.'

'Shh, Sam, please. I need to concentrate on

something,' said Will softly. He closed his eyes and focused all his thoughts on an image from his imagination: a rope bridge made from the living, breathing stems and leaves of the vines. Believe, he repeated to himself, just believe. He pictured the bridge suspended securely from the ceiling across the ravine.

Will heard Sam call out, 'Oh no! Look out. Those vines are moving. Don't let them get me again.'

'It's okay, Sam. It's Will! I think he's doing it. He's controlling the vines!' said Riya in amazement.

Overhead, the great looping, criss-crossing

vines snaked down and knitted themselves purposefully into a neat bridge. 'Whoa! That's incredible!' whooped Sam.

Will opened his eyes and breathed out. His eyes lit up. The bridge was exactly as he had imagined it. 'Yes!' he exclaimed. As the word left his mouth, the vines began to stir. They started to unravel and withdraw back up towards the ceiling.

'Uh-oh,' said Sam. 'Why is that happening?'

Will instantly closed his eyes again and

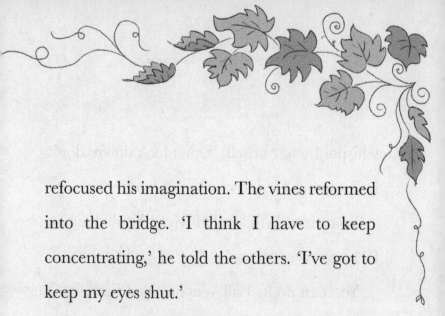

refocused his imagination. The vines reformed into the bridge. 'I think I have to keep concentrating,' he told the others. 'I've got to keep my eyes shut.'

Riya rushed forwards and put her foot on the lowest vine. She pressed her full weight on it, making the bridge bounce up and down slightly. 'It's strong, Will. Keep going. We're going across now.' She leapt onto the bridge and crossed it in a flash.

Sam followed, taking small steps and

whispering to himself, 'Don't look down, don't look down.' He too reached the other side.

'Your turn, Will,' called Riya. 'You'll have to feel your way across.'

'You can do it, Will!' encouraged Sam.

Will reached out and gripped the vines. He felt for the lowest vine with his foot and stepped onto the bridge. Just keep believing, he told himself. He took hesitant steps forwards, feeling his way across the bridge.

'That's it, Will. You're over halfway,' came Riya's voice. Will shuffled his foot forward and shifted his weight onto it. His foot suddenly slipped off the vine into the open air below.

In panic, Will's eyes shot open. He was staring down into the black depths of the ravine. Immediately, the vines around him began to unravel. The rope bridge sagged in the middle. Fear surged to every corner of Will's body. He stumbled forwards clumsily, grasping at the loose vines and missing his step. He could feel the bridge becoming weaker by the second. On the other side, Riya was watching in dismay. She tried to shout encouragement, but her voice caught in her throat.

Sam bellowed to Will, 'Believe, Will! Close your eyes again and believe.'

Riya found her voice again, 'That's right. Persistence is the key, remember!'

All of Will's instincts were urging him to keep moving, but he knew his friends were right. Although the vines were shaking and swaying beneath his feet, Will forced himself to stop moving and close his eyes once more. As he re-imagined the rope bridge, the vines stopped unravelling. However, fear was still pumping through Will's veins and he couldn't hold the image of the bridge stable in his head. He clambered on towards the other side, keeping his eyes shut tight.

'Yes, that's it. Keep imagining it!' cried

Riya. 'It's holding. Just two or three more steps, Will!'

Will could almost sense the end of the bridge and safety. The temptation to look ahead was too much. He opened his eyes and saw he was nearly at the other side, but not as close as Riya had said. The bridge in his imagination was flushed from his mind as a wave of fear swept through him again. The vines began to twist, flop, and break apart.

'Jump!' shouted Riya. Will managed two more quick steps before he was forced to leap out over the terrifying drop. He reached out with his fingers towards the edge. For a moment, Will thought he was going to make it, and then he realized he was dropping too fast. He was about to collide with the sheer rocky wall opposite and tumble into the abyss.

Chapter Seven

As he fell, Will saw Riya cover her mouth in horror and then suddenly he felt as light as a feather. Will was frozen in mid-air inches from the rock face. Warm dribble snaked down the back of his shirt. He could feel Sam's breath ruffling his hair. The young giraffe had caught him just in time. Sam raised his neck and deposited Will gently on the ground next to Riya. Will threw his arms around one of Sam's long legs and hugged him. Before any of them had a chance to speak, large lumps of rock and grit exploded from the wall at the far end of the corridor. **Clicker-clacker!** The Voids poured through the hole triumphantly and marched down the corridor towards them.

The three friends ran up the steps to the next door. As they pushed it closed, Will glanced back to see one of the Voids try to leap across the ravine. As it jumped its fierce red eye was fixed on him, but suddenly it was gone as the Void dropped into the deep ravine. Will breathed a sigh of relief. They were safe again—at least until the Voids found a way across.

Will, Riya, and Sam entered another chamber. Here, the lush plant life from the garden had taken over. The moss sparkled and the flowers bloomed proudly as the light of purple flames danced across the walls and ceilings. It was a magical sight. In the centre of the room was a raised stone platform. And standing on it was a magnificent purple elephant.

'Maji,' whispered Sam in awe.

'You did it, Will,' said Riya. 'We've got through the trials.'

Will rushed forwards, beaming. 'Is she right, Maji?' he asked. 'Have I passed? What happens now? The Voids are close behind.'

Maji's eyes twinkled. 'Yes, Night Zookeeper, you have done all that has been asked of you so far,' she replied.

The smile faded from Will's face. 'So far?' he repeated.

'Will, my ossicones are tingling,' warned Sam suddenly. The ground shuddered under their feet.

'There is one last thing you need to do,' said

Maji. Plaster fell from the ceiling and disintegrated in a puff of dust as it struck the floor.

'Save the temple,' said Will. It was clear what she meant. He had to stop the Voids destroying the temple. 'But how, Maji?' he pleaded.

Maji smiled at him as if there was nothing in the World of Night to worry about. 'You're ready. You're finally ready,' she said.

A sense of surprise and wonder fizzed down the back of Will's neck. 'Grandma?' he whispered to himself. Maji gave him a secret smile.

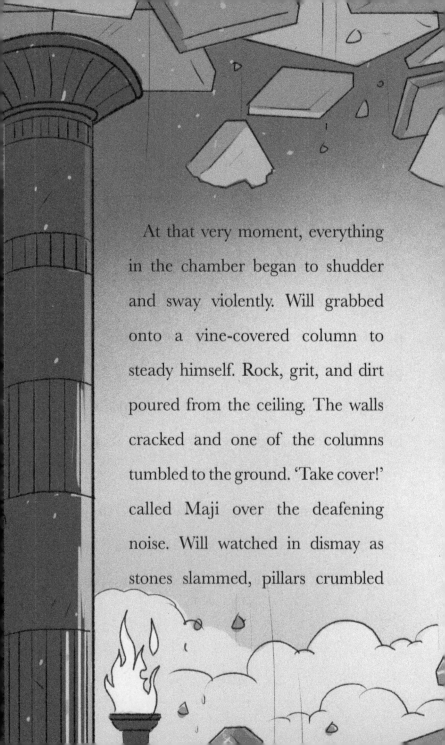

At that very moment, everything in the chamber began to shudder and sway violently. Will grabbed onto a vine-covered column to steady himself. Rock, grit, and dirt poured from the ceiling. The walls cracked and one of the columns tumbled to the ground. 'Take cover!' called Maji over the deafening noise. Will watched in dismay as stones slammed, pillars crumbled

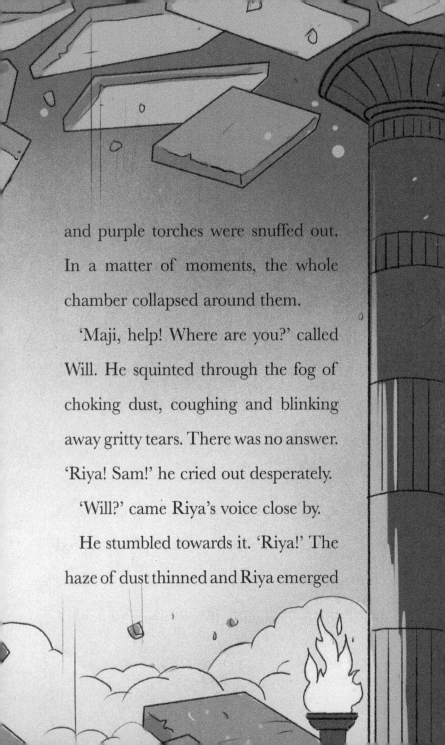

and purple torches were snuffed out. In a matter of moments, the whole chamber collapsed around them.

'Maji, help! Where are you?' called Will. He squinted through the fog of choking dust, coughing and blinking away gritty tears. There was no answer. 'Riya! Sam!' he cried out desperately.

'Will?' came Riya's voice close by.

He stumbled towards it. 'Riya!' The haze of dust thinned and Riya emerged

from the gloom. 'Where's Maji? Sam?'
Suddenly, to Will's surprise, a night sky full of
stars appeared overhead. He gasped. 'Too
late!' he said, his voice hoarse with emotion.
'It's too late. The temple . . .'

'Over there!' exclaimed Riya, pointing. Sam
and Maji stood a little way off, surrounded by
huge hunks of rubble. Will and Riya ran
towards them.

Clicker-clacker! Clicker-clacker!

Will spun towards the metallic gnashing. A
single Void clambered on top of a stunted
column. And then a ring of red lights
surrounded Will and the others. Void after

Void emerged and stood amongst the ruins. Hundreds of crimson eyes stared at the group huddled at the centre of the fallen temple. Silence. A terrible silence, so deep that Will could hear his own pulse throbbing in his ears.

'There's so many,' he said under his breath. 'We can't fight them all!' The Voids stood motionless. 'What are they waiting for?' he whispered, lifting the torch shakily from his pocket.

The Void perched on the smashed column suddenly clanked into life. It thrust its head skyward and a laser beam of red light shot up into the night sky, projecting a terrifying image onto the dark backdrop.

'No,' breathed Will, his heart thudding in his chest. 'Not him!'

A man's face towered over them: a stony face half-covered by a jagged metal mask. Dark eyes bored into them. For a second time, Will felt as if the man's stare were draining the energy from him. He tried to turn away but

then the masked
man's lips curled
at the edges and
parted to reveal a row
of neat teeth. It was the smile of a shark.

'Who . . . who's that, Maji?' stammered
Riya.

Will answered for her, 'It's him, isn't it? It's
the Lord of Nulth!'

A mocking laugh filled the air and then a
scratchy, metallic voice rang out. Will winced.
The sound set his teeth on edge like fingernails
on a blackboard.

'There is no more hiding, Maji,' said the

Lord of Nulth. Maji was staring up at the projection defiantly. 'My Void army has destroyed your temple. The source of all your light and power is gone. Creativity is closed down. Imagination is banished!' Another cruel laugh bombarded Will's senses, dragging him deeper into a sense of despair. 'The Night Zoo is mine for the taking,' gloated Nulth. 'My forces are everywhere, bringing order and obedience to all corners of the World of Night. There is only one job left to do, one I have been looking forward to for a long time.' Nulth paused and glared down at Maji, his eyes glinting with menace. 'Your temple can't save you now. No more time-travelling disappearing acts for you!'

Clicker-clacker! The great circle of Voids burst into a frenzy of fearsome noise.

'Goodbye, Maji,' grinned Nulth. 'The Night Zoo is finished. And now my Voids will finish you. Attack!'

The Voids swarmed towards the friends from all directions.

'What do we do?' cried Sam, his legs quivering.

'All of you, take cover as best you can,' ordered Maji firmly. 'I'll deal with this.' Will and Riya scrambled underneath Maji and

Sam dashed behind a toppled pillar and turned invisible. Maji's eyes flashed with steely determination. She raised her trunk and blasted a ball of crackling purple light at the advancing Voids. Three Voids were struck by the purple blast and collapsed in a heap of fizzing, smoking metal. Maji aimed again and

took out four Voids in one go, their metal shells piling up and blocking the next wave of attackers.

'Behind you!' screamed Sam. Without looking, Maji reared her trunk back over her head and blasted a trio of Voids sneaking up from behind.

'On the left!' shouted Will. *Boom! Clank! Fizzle!*

'Right! Right!' cried Riya. *Blam! Pop! Hiss!*

Will heard Nulth laugh in the sky above: a low, humourless chuckle. He could also hear Maji's laboured breathing and see the heavy thudding of her giant heart against her ribcage. She was tiring, but Will could also see that the Voids were having to slow down to get past the broken ones.

'Keep going!' he urged Maji. 'I believe in you!' Maji trumpeted majestically and hit half a dozen Voids with one purple blast. 'Yes, Grandma—I mean Maji!' shouted Will. Out of the corner of his eye, Will spotted a flash of sleek metal. He jerked his head round and saw it again: a single Void was moving at speed between the fallen rocks and Voids. It dashed left, took cover and then scuttled right behind a chunk of ceiling. He had never seen a Void move so fast. 'Maji, watch out, over there,' he called up to her.

'I see it,' she replied and blasted light from her trunk. To Will's surprise, the Void instantly ducked and the ball of light sailed over its metal back. Maji grunted with annoyance and re-aimed. Again, the Void dodged the blast and the purple ball slammed into a group of other Voids.

'Behind you!' shouted Sam again. Maji was forced to swing her trunk and blast away in the opposite direction. Will kept his eyes on the zigzagging, agile Void. It was closing in on them rapidly. He had no choice. He shot out from underneath the elephant, raised his torch and pressed the button. A bolt of brilliant light shot directly at the speedy Void. At the last moment, it sprang sideways and hunkered down before leaping diagonally behind a pile of broken Voids. Will released the button, but as he did, the Void scuttled forwards and Will fumbled with the torch. The beam of light missed its target again. The Void jumped forwards and hunkered down. *Blast! Miss! Blast! Miss!* Will kept the button held down now, desperately trying to catch the Void in its beam, but it was too quick. Will's fingers, hand, arm, and shoulder shuddered and ached as he concentrated, but his aim was getting worse. He was losing focus and the Void was getting closer by the second. He glanced up at Maji. The infinity symbol of her massive forehead was creased in a deep frown. He looked into her wise eyes and even though she didn't speak, her voice echoed in his head: *Persistence is the key, Will. Watch, learn, and improve.*

Will turned off the torch. He looked up at the crimson image of Nulth towering overhead. The masked man was nodding with approval. 'That's right, Night Zookeeper, give up,' Nulth growled. 'You haven't got it in you. You don't believe. You've never believed in yourself.'

Will ripped his gaze away and refocused on the Void as it scuttled over a rock, hunkered down, and a second later moved on. Watch, Will told himself, don't waste your effort. *Leap, hunker, scurry.* 'Learn,' he said under his breath. *Rush, hunker, jump.* 'And improve,' said Will. He raised the torch and aimed at a spot ahead of the Void. He waited for it to leap. He pressed the button just as the Void landed. He had timed it perfectly. The Void hunkered down for a split second just as Will had anticipated. It was caught in the brilliant beam. 'Gotcha!' he cried. The Void tried to leap out of the way, but it could only stumble forwards. Will kept the beam trained on it but, to his disappointment, it kept moving, more slowly than before but still advancing. The torch shook in Will's hand and he grunted with effort. The Void's metal body was smoking and hissing, yet it was still moving relentlessly closer. 'Oh no you don't!' said Will through gritted teeth. He closed his eyes and let his imagination do the work: he pictured the Void getting smaller, shrinking and shrinking, until it was no larger than a normal spider. Will opened his eyes. Just a few inches from his toes, trapped in the torch beam, was a tiny,

steaming, hissing Void. He switched off the torch. All the other Voids had stopped moving. Silence again. They were watching warily. Will reached down and picked up the tiny, limp Void. He balanced it on his thumb and then casually flicked it away with his forefinger. He smiled triumphantly at the Voids.

'Who's next?' he asked.

Chapter Eight

A **furious** voice filled the air. 'Voids, fall back!' ordered the Lord of Nulth. The remaining Voids began to retreat. Nulth glared down at Maji. 'You may have won this time, Elephant,' he said. 'That boy showed some real spirit. But believe me, the next time we meet, I will crush that spirit from him. And he will follow me!'

'Never!' shouted Will. 'I'll never be like you, you miserable, grey bully!' The projected image of Nulth fizzled out and the last Void left the ruins of the temple. Will found that his fists were clenched and his legs were shaking. He looked around at the devastation of the battle: the broken pillars, the smashed stones, the crushed plants and flowers and the broken, silent Voids. A sickly feeling gripped his stomach.

Sam galloped out from his hiding place. 'You did it, Will!'

Riya emerged from underneath Maji and gave him a quick hug. 'That was amazing. Will

. . . what's wrong?'

Will's eyes filled with tears. 'I didn't do anything,' he said, his voice catching. 'Look around. There's nothing left, just piles of stones and broken Voids. I'm sorry, Maji: I failed the last trial, didn't I?'

Maji raised her trunk and placed the tip gently on Will's shoulder. 'Now why in the World of Night would you think that?' she asked with a mysterious smile.

'I don't understand,' said Will, confused. 'The temple. I had to save the temple. And it's gone. I don't deserve to be the Night Zookeeper.'

Maji lowered her head and looked Will square in the eye. 'Will, there's something you must understand,' she said. 'Saving the temple was never one of your trials. The real trial was to use all that you have learnt about never giving up, bravery, and concentration to make the most of your imagination. The real trial was to save me. And here I am, safe and sound, thanks to you.'

Will blinked away his tears. 'But your beautiful temple . . .' he mumbled.

'It doesn't matter,' Maji replied. 'Will, the Lord of Nulth thought that if he destroyed the temple, he would destroy all that we hold dear:

imagination, curiosity, and free thought. He was wrong, because the temple is not home to these things: it's just a bunch of stones, after all.' Maji placed the tip of her trunk on Will's chest. 'No, Will, the real home of these things is here. Inside you. That spark of creativity is alive, thriving and safe inside you. And when you fuel that spark with persistence, well, then you get something very special indeed.

It's why I chose you to be the Night Zookeeper and it's why you have passed the trials with flying colours.'

A warm glow of happiness and pride filled Will's chest. He beamed at Maji.

'Yes!' exclaimed Riya. Sam, whose big eyes were glistening, sniffed a couple of times.

'It is time for you all to continue your journey,' said Maji. 'Thank you, Riya. Thank you, Sam. Your friendship with Will only makes all of you stronger. And now I must continue my journey too. The Lord of Nulth will be plotting his next move and I must be ready.'

'But can't we travel with you?' asked Will, a lump forming in his throat.

Maji shook her huge head slowly. 'Not this time, Night Zookeeper. You must continue your adventures without me.' The infinity symbol on Maji's head burst into light and her enormous purple body shimmered.

'Wait, please don't go,' Will whispered.

'Remember, Will, persistence is the key,' she said. She was fading from sight. She kept her wise, twinkling eyes on Will. Her voice filled the night air, 'And all you have to do is believe.'

Will, Riya, and Sam stood alone in the quiet ruins of the temple.

'Well, what now?' asked Riya quietly.

Will shook his head. Now Maji had gone, he suddenly felt small and unsure again. 'I really don't know,' he said.

'Knock, knock,' said Sam.

'Not now, Sam,' said Riya.

'Knock, knock,' insisted Sam.

'Who's there?' Will replied.

'Stopwatch.'

'Stopwatch who?'

'Stopwatch you're doing and look at this!' Sam said. Will gasped. The ground around their feet was alive. Will's heart flew into his mouth: huge green snakes were writhing amongst the ruins of the temple. And then he realized they weren't snakes at all. It was the Silent Creepers.

'What are they doing?' asked Riya.

Will watched as two creepers slowly pulled a pillar upright and others placed a huge stone on top of another. 'I think they're rebuilding it!' he said in amazement. 'They're putting the temple back together.'

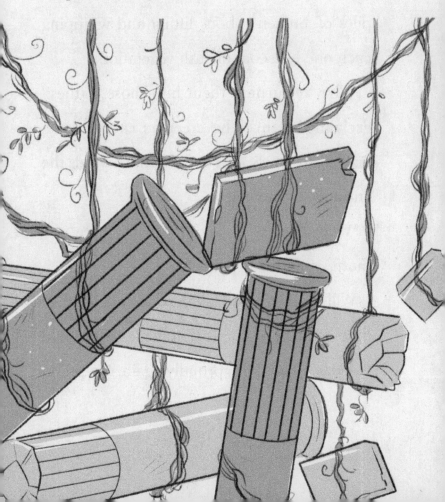

'The Voids,' said Riya suddenly. 'Look what they're doing to the Voids.' They stared in fascination as the creepers swept over the piles of broken robots, lifting and wrapping each one in a coat of lush vegetation.

'They're turning them into those statues!' exclaimed Sam. The creepers carried each leafy Void slowly over the ground towards the entrance to the maze.

'Well, I guess we're not needed here any more,' remarked Riya.

Will nodded and smiled. It would take time, but he was happy that the temple would one day stand there proudly again. He raised his torch.

'Ready, guys?'

'Ready!' chorused Riya and Sam.

Will drew a huge infinity symbol in the night sky. Another landscape slowly emerged on the other side of the portal: it was a huge, jagged, icy mountain.

'Whoa,' said Riya. 'That is so cool and so weird.'

'I've heard of this place,' said Sam excitedly. 'It's called the Mountain in the Sky.'

Will gazed at the spectacular scene. The mountain was indeed floating in the sky. A beautiful frozen waterfall jutted from the

edge of the mountain down towards the ground far below. Will stepped forwards, followed by his two best friends, through the portal and into a new adventure.

About the Author

By night, Joshua Davidson is the head Night Zookeeper. He works in the Night Zoo and cares for many magical animals such as purple octocows and banana hedgehogs. During his nightly rounds he enjoys playing memory games with the time-travelling elephant and hide and seek with the spying giraffes. Sadly he is yet to win a single game in either contest.

By day, he is an author, artist, game designer and tech entrepreneur. He came up with the idea for nightzookeeper. com, a website where anyone can draw animals and write stories about them, whilst studying an MA in Digital Art at Norwich University of the Arts.

Josh introduced the Night Zoo to Paul, Buzz, Phil and Sam and together they built the Night Zookeeper website, which has since been nominated for a BAFTA, won a London Book Fair award and is currently used in thousands of schools across the world to inspire amazing creative writing.

About the Illustrator

Buzz studied graphic design in Norwich, England where he met Night Zookeeper Josh. Many years later, Josh brought Buzz to the gates of the Night Zoo. Ever since then he has been the regular painter and decorator in the zoo. He draws on his gigantic imagination to care for the animals there and to explore new, previously uncharted parts of the world!

By day, Buzz Burman is a designer and illustrator with a love of clever ideas. As well as drawing what the animals look like in this book, he also designed the cover, the Night Zookeeper website and Night Zookeeper logo!

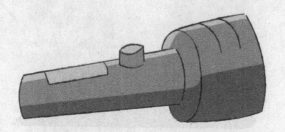

Maji's Memory Game

Did you know that elephants never forget?
This is especially true of time-travelling
elephants like Maji! Here's how to play her
favourite memory game.

1-4 players

Instructions

1. Look at all of the different animal names below for 1 minute.

Lion, Tiger, Snake, Elephant, Giraffe, Penguin, Flamingo, Sea Lion, Crocodile, Bear, Eagle, Monkey, Panda, Dolphin, Whale

2. Close the book.

3. On a separate piece of paper, write down as many animals as you can! (No peeking!)

4. Score yourself out of 15.

5. If you are playing with family and friends, the player with the top score wins!

Want to play again? Simply get a piece of paper and write down 15 new animal names. Then repeat the above instructions!

Sam's Maze

Night Zookeeper Will has used his torch to shrink Sam! Can you help him to get to the centre of the maze? Remember, persistence is the key!

Splodge

By quietstarfish43, Year 6, UK

My name is Splodge and I have been said to have a very bright and energetic personality so I'm constantly flapping around showing off my yellow and pink splodges. I have lived in the magnificent Night Zoo since I was born and I have been known to be a bit of a show off.

This year I chose to do a sponsored fly to raise money for

the amazing charity Red Cross. I also helped them teach others the important skill of first aid. Helping out at charities makes me feel overwhelmingly good and I think everyone should try it.

At the Night Zookeeper's party I will wear my sparkling jacket so I'll really stand out from the crowd! Excitedly, me and my friends have been busily getting ready, discussing the party. I am so excited! It is going to be awesome!

I love singing and dancing because I can be different from everyone else and have some fun. I'm not very good at camouflage so the game I dislike the most is hide and seek, because I'm always found. I much rather play tag where we fly around and tag each other.

My best friends name is Sonny. Even though we're exact opposites (Sonny is silent and shy) we are inseparable. We are always having sleepovers and I couldn't imagine my life without him.

The Flying Pig Learns How to Oink

By Palepig71, Year 5, UK

Once upon a time, in a large, grassy farm yard, there was a big, fat, pink pig. All day long, the pig lay around the yard, lazily gazing up at the birds in the sky, wondering what it would be like to fly. One day, he decided it was time to stop watching and start doing! He was going to try and fly himself. He was going to succeed, it was inevitable! He already had a plan in his head, but he would need some help. First of all he asked Horsey to kick out one of the planks of wood from the fence. After that, he asked Cow to turn over the water trough.

Finally, he got Chicken to climb up the tree ready to jump down. Everything was ready! Using the plank and the upside down water trough, he built a seesaw and stood on one end.

'GO!' he shouted to Chicken excitedly. She jumped down onto the other end of the plank with great expectation. But nothing happened. She was not heavy enough to make Pig fly.

'Quick, everyone, climb the tree together,' announced Pig to the others. So up went chicken and horse and cow together.

Pig counted them down from five and they all leapt off the branch at once, landing on the plank with a THUMP. The piece of wood pivoted on the water trough and up into the air Pig flew. He had done it, he was actually flying! Pig's thrilling ride lasted a few seconds before he realised his mistake. How do you land from flying? UH OH . . .

Night Zookeeper uses storytelling
and technology to encourage creativity and
imagination. Our magical stories inspire
traditional creative play and develop reading,
writing, and drawing skills.

We believe in fairness and offer free
digital education products to all children
around the world.

Thank you for buying this book
and supporting our mission.

Visit **nightzookeeper.com**
for more information.

The Giraffes of
Whispering Wood

When Will accidentally creates a mysterious portal during a trip to the zoo, he's transported into the world of the Night Zoo, and thrust into an incredible adventure.

Bestowed with a zookeeper's uniform, a mysterious orb, and a powerful magical torch, he's tasked with protecting the Zoo's inhabitants from the fearsome Voids—the army of robotic spiders who are terrorizing the Spying Giraffes that live there.

Does Will, with the help of his friend Riya, have the bravery and the imagination to lead the creatures of the Night Zoo to victory?

The Lioness of
Fire Desert

Joined by his friends, Sam and Riya, Will journeys to Fire Desert, where rumours of a mysterious creature called 'the Grip' have struck fear into the hearts of the animals. Even Captain Claw, a fierce lioness, is acting strangely on hearing the news.

The animals look to Will to save them, but can he find the bravery he needs to step up to the challenge, or will fear hold him back?

The Penguins of
Igloo City

Joined by his friends, Sam and Riya, Will journeys to the eerie Igloo City. It is a strange place where the animals follow strict rules made by their leader, Circles the owl. Circles is determined to stamp out any rule breakers and wants Will to track down a group of troublesome rebels.

The safety of Igloo City depends on Will making the right choice: should he follow Circles' orders or disobey them by joining the rebels?

The Zoo Needs You!

Continue your adventure on
nightzookeeper.com

Create your own magical animals

Defeat
evil Voids

Rescue Sam the Spying Giraffe